Don't Be Afraid of the Storm

Connie Caban

Illustrated by Gen Page

the Peppertree Press
Sarasota, Florida

P9-CNG-385

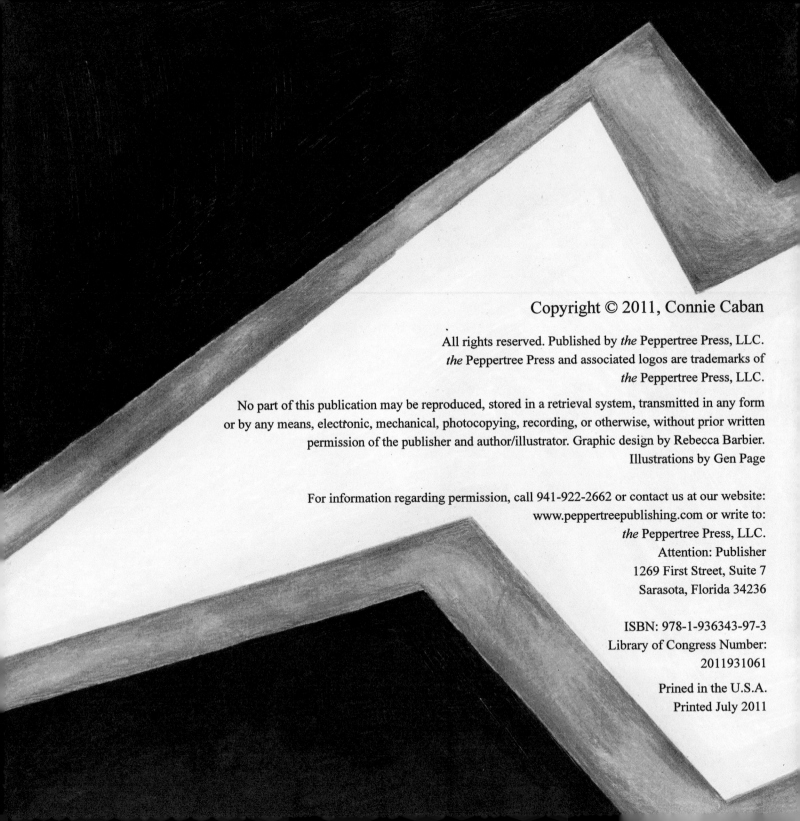

For information regarding permission, call 941-922-2662 or contact us at our website:
www.peppertreepublishing.com or write to:
the Peppertree Press, LLC.
Attention: Publisher
1269 First Street, Suite 7
Sarasota, Florida 34236

ISBN: 978-1-936343-97-3
Library of Congress Number:
2011931061

Prined in the U.S.A.
Printed July 2011

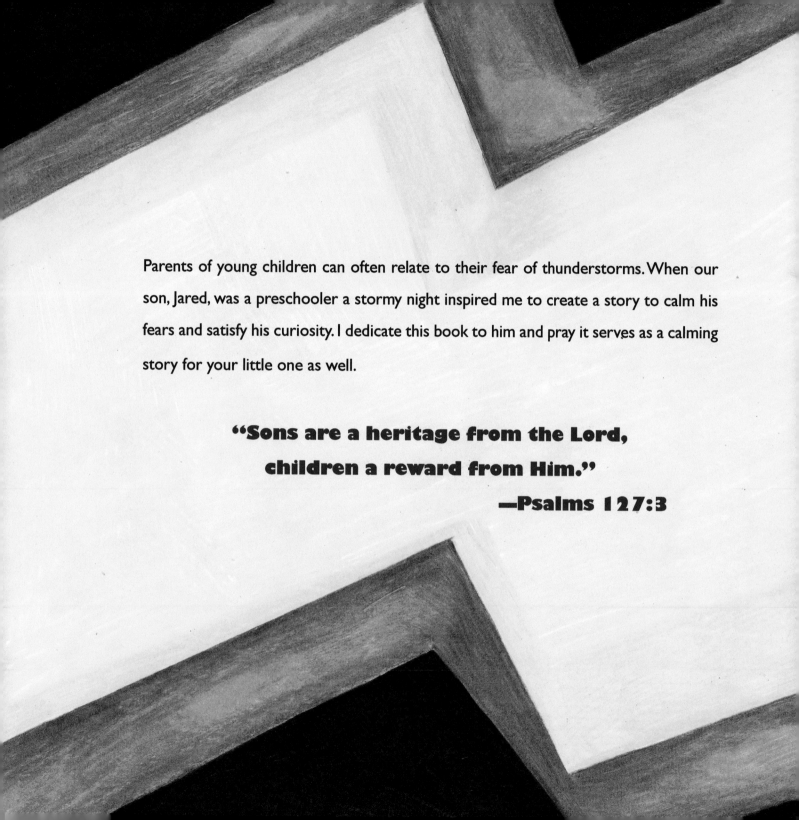

Parents of young children can often relate to their fear of thunderstorms. When our son, Jared, was a preschooler a stormy night inspired me to create a story to calm his fears and satisfy his curiosity. I dedicate this book to him and pray it serves as a calming story for your little one as well.

"Sons are a heritage from the Lord, children a reward from Him."

—Psalms 127:3

The thunderstorm was very loud!
Jared heard his puppy, Tiki,
crying from under his bed.

5

"Can I sleep with you?"

Daddy reached out and put his arms around Jared giving him a big hug.

"Don't be afraid of the storm, son. Remember, it's only God watering His gardens."

Holding Jared's hand,
Daddy led him back
to his room.
**"Let's get you and
Tiki back to bed.
Maybe we'll play ball
tomorrow."**

8

"Good night, Jared."

"Good night, Daddy."

Safe again beneath his warm covers, Jared knew Daddy was right. He slowly closed his eyes and tried to sleep.

Mommy awoke and gently pulled Jared onto the bed.

"What's wrong, honey?"
she asked wiping tears from his eyes.

**"The storm is SCARING me!
Just listen, Mommy!"**

12

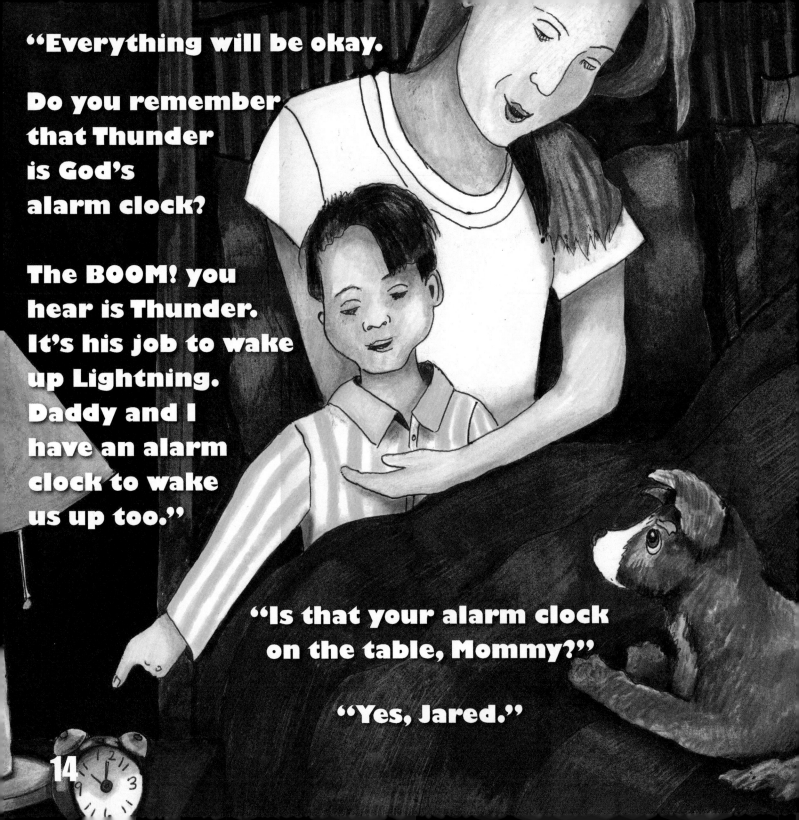

"Everything will be okay.

Do you remember that Thunder is God's alarm clock?

The BOOM! you hear is Thunder. It's his job to wake up Lightning. Daddy and I have an alarm clock to wake us up too."

"Is that your alarm clock on the table, Mommy?"

"Yes, Jared."

14

"Thunder BOOMS! and wakes up Lightning.
The CRAAACK! and BANG! you hear are
Lightning turning on the lights so
God can see to water His beautiful
gardens with rain.

We turn on lights so
we can see too."

"God created Thunder and Lightning to help Him water His creation."

19

Jared felt better now. Mommy carried him to his room and gently tucked him into bed.

"Good night, Jared," she whispered kissing his cheek. **"Go back to sleep. I'll see you in the morning."**

20

Jared snuggled beneath his covers
with Tiki curled up next to him.
But, before he could even close his
eyes he heard another...

21

Shaking, he sprang from his bed running this time to big brother Gabriel's room. Tiki followed at his heels barking loudly.

"Gabe! Gabe! I'm SCARED! Aren't you?"

23

Gabriel awoke and sleepily rubbed his eyes.

**"No, not really. Don't be scared, Jared.
It's only God watering His gardens."**

Gabe heard Mommy and Daddy
tell the story many times before.

"Just go back to bed. You'll be okay."

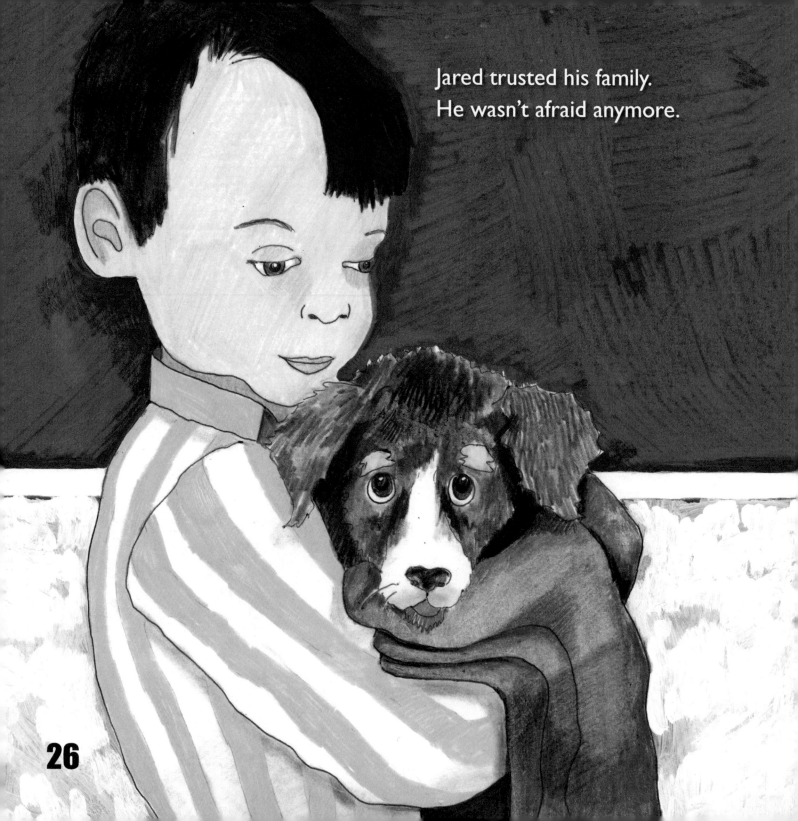

Jared trusted his family.
He wasn't afraid anymore.

26

Walking back to his room and holding
Tiki close, he whispered,

**"It's okay, Tiki, don't
be afraid of the storm.
It's only God watering
His gardens."**

He climbed into bed and snuggled
with Tiki beneath the warm covers.

Thunder **BOOMED!**
Lightning **CRAAACKED!**
And Lightning **BANGED!**

...but the two soon fell fast asleep.

"Without warning a furious storm came up. You of little faith, why are you so afraid? Jesus rebuked the winds and waves and it was calm. Even the winds and waves obey Him."

— Matthew 8:24-27

CPSIA information can be obtained
at www.ICGtesting.com
Printed in the USA
247755LV00004BC

9781936343973